How the Adult Angles Wanted to Cancel Christmas

BOOKS on DEMAND

In loving memory of my mother

Rosel Schwaigert

We miss you

Axel Schwaigert

How the Adult Angles Wanted to Cancel Christmas

Christmas stories for children and adults

Bibliografische Information
der Deutschen Nationalbibliothek:
Die Deutsche Nationalbibliothek verzeichnet diese
Publikation in der Deutschen Nationalbibliografie;
detaillierte bibliografische Daten sind im Internet über
http://dnb.dnb.de abrufbar.

Illustration: Isabell Hemming

Herstellung und Verlag:
BoD – Books on Demand, Norderstedt
ISBN 978-3-8448-0769-1

Thank you

I want to say thank you to everybody who helped that this little book became a reality. Thank you to Isabell for the wonderful little drawings and her creativity.

Thank you to my family for their support. A special thank you to my brother for nagging me again and again, asking: "How is you book project doing?"

Thank you to Mary Smail, Mia Brirggs, Andrea Offner and Ken Dimmick for helping to transform my text into real English.

Thank you to my teachers at Episcopal Divinity School for encouraging me to express my thoughts in stories.

And a thank you to my congregation, Salz der Erde MCC Gemeinde Stuttgart, for letting me tell these stories in our Christmas service in the first place. Thank you all.

A Short Introduction

Thousands of dusty volumes of sermons line the shelves of seminary libraries all around the world. And I say dusty because nobody every pulls them down to read. Printed volumes of sermons almost make we want to reevaluate whether or not the printing press was really a good thing. I would go so far as to say that printed sermons are unreadable and unhelpful. Call the sermons essays and maybe I would give them more value. But sermons are a speaking art. There should be pulpits involved, and clergy vested according to their own traditions, and...most importantly, a congregation of interested people who are actually paying the preacher to preach. The cling on his every word. The skill of his vocal technique brings life to the scholarly and inspiring words.

So if all this is how I see volumes of sermons, why you might ask am I writing a foreword to this new volume of sermons from the Rev. Dr. Axel Schwaigert? The answer is simple. These are not really sermons. Yes, I know they were written as sermons, and delivered before Dr. Schwaigert's congregation, who clung to his every word, but they are something much more than sermons. They are stories with homiletical background.

Growing up in Germany, Dr. Schwaigert represents the culture that brought the world the Grimm's Fairly Tales, Wagner's Ring Cycle, and countless myths and legends from the witch infested Black Forest to haunted Harz Mountains. Dr. Schwaigert knows that the greatest truths far exceed human language's ability to express it with clarity. Metaphor, irony, and hyperbole are needed to bring us anywhere close to the truth of such infinite subjects as God, Christ, Salvation, and Love.

This wonderful volume of "sermon-stories" offers the listener or now that they are printed, the reader, the chance to enter into the childlike world where cows can talk and angels can pout. The point is not to avoid the big serious issues, but to talk about big and serious issues in ways which bring new light to the murkiness we theologians and parish clergy find ourselves. When reading these "sermon-stories" we don't fall asleep. We don't wring our hands in panic trying to remember our classical Greek declensions. We don't argue with the writer and slam the book against the wall. But we do smile. We might laugh. We definitely pursue the plot to the very last word, before uttering our own joyous Amen. Thanks be to God.

Read these stories and enjoy. That is definitely what Dr. Schwaigert would want. Read these stories and meditate on what they say, and what they don't say. Just read them for yourself or to others and later read them again. The perfect antidote to dusty scholarly shelf-fillers.

The Rev. Canon Kenneth Dimmick
St. Catherine's Anglican Church Stuttgart

How the Adult Angles
Wanted to Cancel Christmas

It was already a few days before Christmas, and the mood in heaven was extremely bad. The angels were angry: there was no way they would continue! There was a storm building among the angels. Even the clouds, on which the angels normally played their harps, looked more like a distant thunderstorm. Gabriel, the head-angel finally called a general assembly of all the angels and saints, so they could discuss the problem. All the famous, and not so famous saints came. From the strong Guardian angles with their huge, white wings to the most fragile music angel all where there.

The first speaker made a point: "The humans on earth don't deserve Christmas! Instead of being joyful and meditating on the season they are focused on consumerism and hectic racing around. Instead of peace on earth, they have fights under the Christmas tree and wars all over the place. Why should they get to celebrate a holiday which seems to be important only for the retail industry?"

"Exactly!" the next angel agreed. She was the one who was responsible for the weather. "First, they dream about a white Christmas, with jingle bells and sleigh rides, and perfectly white Hollywood snow. But when we give them snow, they complain about the temperature and the traffic chaos! And on top of that: Global warming is their own fault. And can

anybody explain what romance in front of a fire place
has to do with Christmas?"

"I totally agree" grumbled the holy bishop Nicolas
of Myra. "They reduce me to somebody who brings
presents and now I am just a poster guy advertising a
certain sweet American soft drink… just can't
remember the name…"

"Yes," interrupted Saint Augustine, the chief
theologian and Father of the Church, "Humans no
longer even know about the structure of the calendar
year of the church! And if you ask anybody on the
street about the meaning of "Incarnation theology"!
Nobody knows! They just scratch their heads. It is the
most important term in systematic theology and …"

The rest of his lecture was shouted down in a
general clamor that sounded something like this: "The
humankind does not care about real meaning of

Christmas anymore! They do not even deserve Christmas! And the best would be if the angels just would decide to do away with Christmas altogether!" Gabriel, one of the big angels finally summed it up by concluding that Christmas seemed to be useless for the humans anyhow. So the angels and saints might as well use the time, as the humans did - take a nice vacation somewhere in the sunny south. Hawaii or the Bahamas are very nice this time of year.

While a fight started at the gathering of angels and saints about where they should go for a Christmas vacation, three little angels were sitting to the side and were all puzzled. They had listened to the adults and did not understand at all why they were so upset or what the fighting was all about. In their opinion Christmas was such an important celebration. It was so beautiful. They had tried to speak up, but none of the adults had listened to them. They tried to speak about love, and peace, about courage and hope but the arguing was too loud.

That the adults wanted to do away with Christmas... the little angels could not believe it. Sad, they folded their halos and left with hanging wings. On a out-of-the-way cloud they sat down and thought about what they could do. To talk to the adult angles was out of the question. That simply would not work. Adults never listened. They could go directly to God, and head to the heavenly throne. But they did not have the courage to do that.

But, then they got another idea: they could go down to the humans themselves and bring them the real Christmas. Yes, that was something they could do! And if the adults did not want to help, then the little angels would do it all by themselves! Each one of them would fly down to earth, carrying only what they had recently learned in their short existence as angels. They said, "Let the adults fight if they want!"

And so, the three little angels headed out the bring Christmas to the humans on earth. They started out together and once they landed on earth, each of them choose a direction. So off they went!

Now, everyone knows that each angel has a special task, a job they are especially well prepared for. The most famous ones of all were of course the guardian angels. All the little angels dreamed about being as big and strong as them one day. They all wanted to learn Judo and Karate and things like that to be able to protect the humans.

But of course there are many more jobs and tasks in heaven. And so, the first little angel that secretly flew out of heaven was an angel of love. He was a little chubby and unimpressive for the most part. But those who can see with their hearts could see that the little angel of love had beautifully coloured wings. And so he flew with his coloured wings over the grey roofs of a city.

One house was as grey as another, but one of them was especially grey. On the spur of the moment he stopped and entered. Inside he found an old couple, sitting there in cold silence. As it was the same on all other holidays this Christmas, too, they just existed next to each other. They were not really in a fight with each other, but also not really in peace. They lived in a grey world of daily routine, of habit. The love between them had become cold and had withered away in the troubles and worries of the years and boredom. Mournful, the angle looked around. He saw nothing that could have helped, only greyness.

But then he looked with angel-vision a small speck of colour was hidden somewhere in a cupboard. It was an old photo album, left over from a time when people still put photos in books. He took it out of the drawer and silently placed it between the couple onto the table. They had long ago forgotten about this album, and they were a little surprised that just today they happened to come across it. There were pictures of their youth, when they just had met, two Flower-power kids dancing at a concert under the moon. They had been barefoot hippies in the dew, and they remembered how they had fallen in love that night and how they kissed for the first time. They looked at each other and the *love*, which had become so grey and dusty, came back to them.

The angel could see it quite clearly: it was not the hot, first love of yonder youthful nights, and it also was not the romantic and hopeful love of the early years together. It was a love that had grown and had become older with them. And they felt a deep intimacy with each other and they decided, for the first time in many years, that they would go out and buy a Christmas tree. And together they would decorate it with the colours of their memories.

The second angel just flew around without any particular aim. He was vivid! Yes, he was an angel of peace with large white wings of a dove. But today he did not feel peaceful at all. He was furious with the adult angels, especially with what they had said about snow. Stupid snow! What in heaven has snow to do with peace on earth, or with Christmas? Nothing? And so he decided to fly somewhere, where there was no snow whatsoever, and no Christmas.

He finally reached a little village, somewhere in a dessert. He saw that there were two houses, with a dead tree right on the borderline between them. The tree had died because of the conflict and hatred between the two men who lived there. Every day the fought and called each other names, and sometimes they threw with stones and garbage at each other. Silently the little angel of peace sat on that tree. He knew, he was too small to bring peace on earth or reconciliation between people.

All the angels in heaven were not strong enough to do that. Only the humans themselves could do that. But perhaps he could bring some peace to those two men, who came from different people sand religions and yet in truth - were brothers. While he sat there and thought about it, the dead tree could feel that he was there and it brought forth leaves and tiny blossoms, white and fragrant and fragile.

The two men came out of their houses and saw the almond blossoms and they understood. For the first time in years they did not yell but greeted each other. And for the first time they could hear, that "Shalom" sounds just like "Salam" and means "Peace". And they went and fetched some chairs and sat down next to each other in their garden and together they rejoiced in the miracle of life. And the small angel sat there and rejoiced with them. He had not seen that the name on the sign at the entrance to the little village was "Bethlehem" and that this little peace was perhaps a much larger peace after all.

The third angel decided to fly to a place where people usually think they can find Christmas. He flew straight to the largest Christmas Market he could find. All over the place there were Christmas Carols, the smell of roasted almonds and mulled wine, candles and mistletoe. But in reality it was just fast paced, loud and full of people, pushing and shoving. He was sure he would find something he could do as a young heralding angel with a trumpet.

When he had landed, though, with his used trumpet, he was not quite as confident as he had been. After all he was only in the beginner's class for future horn-playing angels, and the truth was: He could not really play yet. Actually he only knew one Christmas song so far, and he had still problems in some parts. How should he bring Christmas to the people with that? It just would not work. And even if he could play, the market was just too crowded and too loud and too gaudy.

What had sounded like a good plan back in heaven, 'to just bring Christmas to the people', well, down here on earth it looked totally different. The little trombone angel lost all his courage. He just wanted to fly off when he saw, over on the other side of the market, a young boy standing alone. He had a music stand in front of him and, just like the little angel, a used trumpet in his hand. Yet he did not play. The little angel pushed his way through, and saw: it was his song that the boy had in front of him. And so he took a deep breath, took all his little angel courage together, nudged the boy in the side and together they played... the perhaps worst rendition of "Silent night" ever performed.

In the hustle and bustle of the Christmas Market barely anyone heard them. Only a mother of a small three year old child stood there for a moment of peace in midst of the hectic Market. She smiled. It sounded horrible, but in some way it also was beautiful, to see those two children standing there, tooting bravely into their instruments. She looked down at her own son, and saw, that he was totally spellbound. She nearly missed as he said, with big eyes and full of wonder: "When I am tall, I want to do that, too!" And she knew: at that moment, Christmas had happened.

Meanwhile, up in heaven the debate about the bad treatment of Christmas by the humans continued after the small angels had flown off.

Suddenly it became brighter … and more quiet … and a lot more peaceful. The angels and the saints fell silent. Jesus himself entered their midst. Just as it has been his habit since the resurrection, he just had appeared right there among them. And in the silence that happened, everyone could hear his deep sigh. The angels and the saints immediately knew that they had gone too far and had misbehaved. And they fully expected a heavenly telling off. But instead Jesus just smiled and said: "Oh ye angels and saints! You are just too perfect. Which is the reason why you are in heaven, after all. And now you think everything must be as perfect as you are, and everybody needs to understand what Christmas is and how to celebrate it like you do. The people on earth are not as perfect as you are. The humans live in stressful times and in conflict, in unhappiness and they are often faint hearted. And still they can see Christmas in their own way, if they just look closely enough." He smiled. "Especially you, Gabriel, you should know this better than all the others. Don´t you remember, how you came to my mother Mary that day, and told her that she would be pregnant with me? Don´t you remember the fear in her heart, and the fight she had with Josef when she told him that she was with child? Don't you remember the stress and the difficulties and the

17

dejection they felt when they could not find a inn that night. And you surely remember that there was war in many parts of the world in those days. And still Christmas happened. All you angels were there and sang about peace on earth. The wise ones from the east came and the shepherds were there, too."

"I want to show you, how Christmas can come for the people on earth." And in front of him the heaven opened and a bright beam of light fell down on earth, just as the sun sometimes shines through the dark clouds of a storm. And in this light the angels and the saints saw what the little angels had done. They watched as they sat on their cloud, making plans, and how they flew down to bring a little bit of Christmas to the people.

Now the other angels were really quiet and the saints were very embarrassed. In all their anger, that Christmas was not just the way they wanted it to be for themselves they missed something. As they argued about how it could be perfect and theologically correct, they totally had forgotten what Christmas really was: Those small moments of peace, of quietness, of love and of music. All those moments that together make the gift that God gave to the people on earth at Christmas time: Celebrating the birth of Jesus for all the people.

Jesus smiled as he saw how the angels and saints began to understand. And he said to them: "You can prepare the perfect Christmas here in heaven, if you want. But I will now go down to earth as I have done every year, every day and every moment, and just as I did that night some 2000 years ago. I will be with the people, wherever they let me in, and wherever they give me room amongst them; where the wise pray together with all the others and know, they are not different; where gifts are not measured in their value, but in the love in which they are given; where people love each other, console each other, work for peace, give each other courage. It will be Christmas again" He smiled: "... weather you adult angels like it, or not."

Clarence, the Messenger Angel

He was mad! He was simply furious! No, actually, he was hurt and even angry. Yes, that's what he was – angry! Clarence, freshly licensed Messenger Angel, flew over a meadow of clouds and angrily kicked a few small banks of cloud. He had worked and laboured and now, this was the result! They were sending him to shepherds! "Tell them about the birth", they had said! Ha!

Again he lost his temper and kicked a piece of cloud which was sticking out right in front of him. He was so angry that he had not noticed the peak of a high mountain which was arising out of the clouds. He had just hit it with his right foot. Ouch! If he wasn't an angel, and one with a thorough education in communications, he would have used some highly inappropriate language. As it was, he just sat down, held his hurting foot in his hands and sulked.

Week after week he had worked. He had taken classes, sat through endless lectures and very often after his daily choir practice, and on top of his usual job, he had studied for the exams – the Finals. Actually, it had paid off. He had finished his post-graduate degree with honours. Clarence, M.A. - "Messenger Angel". He had been examined in "Public appearance and free speech", and in

"Liturgical Hebrew, Greek and Latin". He had submitted many papers, including one about "The rendition of divine truth and bible content". He had been orally examined on "The history of annunciation theory". His final thesis was titled "Famous messenger angels and important prophets - the importance of inter-personal relationships in the promulgation of meaning." He had also gone to the lengths of taking a theatre class, to learn to control his stage fright. It all went well. He had passed all his exams, and his professors had been very proud of him. After all this work, he had really hoped to get a good assignment, especially now this once in eternity opportunity had come along. But no!

OK, it was a done deal that Gabriel, the Archangel himself had got the job to do the annunciation to Mary, the mother of the saviour – no surprise there, but that they had given Clarence this unimportant and insultingly insignificant task that was … He was lost for words.

When the COC, the Christmas Organisation Committee, had called him, he had so hoped for a good appointment. He wanted to tell the birth of the saviour to important people. That was why he had worked so hard! He wanted to tell prime people - like priests in the temple, or the multitude of people in Jerusalem, or one of the significant prophets! Or they could have sent him to Rome or Athens. After all, he had studied Latin and Greek and knew how to speak to pagans! Even something small and creative would have done.   They could have commissioned him to speak to Joseph in a dream and give him the name of the new-born.   Joseph should know the name; he was the stand-in father, after all.

If he was really honest with himself, Clarence had seen himself standing over a frightened and shaking crowd of people, with his wings spread out, his garments brightly white, shining with all the Glory of God. He had imagined himself speaking the holy words of annunciation in a thundering voice. Those words!   Generations of children would learn them by heart – all quoting Clarence the Messenger Angel. But this!

"There will be shepherds, abiding in the field" they had said, "keeping watch over their flock by night. Go and tell them, that this day, in the city of David, the saviour is born".

That was it. He wouldn't have to take extra equipment, no microphone or loudspeaker. He was to appear to five people, six at the most, and there certainly would be no need for a prepared and rehearsed text. They said he must be sure that he got there on time and he must be ready to start. They told him that as an angel he would know the right moment to begin.

And so Clarence sat on his cloud, holding his sore foot and feeling very disappointed. No spread wings, no multitude of people, no theatrical thunder –just a few uneducated, un-important shepherds. How could he ever meet his colleagues who had probably been given all the posh and fancy, important tasks? They would never openly laugh at him, but he already could hear them saying, "Clarence, this is a vital service to the public!" And, "Size in congregations doesn't matter!"

Then they would tell him where they were being sent, and all about the great, important and creative things they had been given to do.

NO! He would not do this to himself. Instead, he would set out right away, and would spend time somewhere down on earth until it was time for the birth. Clarence made his way to a heavenly storeroom and found an old coat and a shabby hat. These clothes covered his halo and the wings, even if they were old and ragged, and smelled a bit. He put on the clothes and started out to earth.

The shepherds were easy to find. They sat around the one lit fire outside the small village where the miracle would soon happen. They were five down-and-out figures sitting around a fire that night. Clarence could have just waited somewhere in the dark, but what harm could it do, if he went and sat with them? He began to move towards them.

The shepherds became aware of somebody approaching through the darkness. Cautiously they reached for their staffs and clubs that were always within easy reach, for such an occasion. When they saw that it was someone as poor and ragged as they were, they put their weapons away. The stranger said he had lost his way. They welcomed him and yes, of course he could stay by the fire till morning came. Of course, he could sit down and there was some bean-stew left, not much, but he should take it. As the silent stranger sat next to them with his bowl of beans, they slowly started their conversation again.

Clarence sat there and listened carefully. It was a mundane conversation. It revolved around the smaller and larger worries of the shepherds. They talked about their fear of being drafted into the Roman army, until one of them remarked bitterly that not even the Roman army would want people like them. A female shepherd spoke about love and her boyfriend problems – he was a goatherd from the other side of the village, and he had not been in contact with her for over one and a half days! They talked about the latest model of shepherds staffs, and how they would never be able to afford them, not in difficult times like these. And they went on about not being able to trust politicians, and those who had all the money - those crooks were only concerned with power, and not with the good of the people.

A mundane conversation, really. But Clarence, the educated communications angel that he was, heard what they really said. It was the smaller and lager problems of daily life. They had a deep mistrust against all that was presented to them as truth from outside, or from above. The powerful people could not be believed. They were only playing their own games and did not care at all about the common people, like shepherds. He heard about the fear of the future; a future that would be even worse than the present. It was not a light conversation, all in all there was nothing uplifting spoken about in that night around the fire. How should he, Clarence, now declare an eternal truth, something that didn't seem to connect with the lives of those ordinary people at all? And how should they believe him, if they did not believe in anything anymore?

But as he still listened and thought about what he had heard, Clarence, the messenger angel, sensed that it was time. Somewhere in the village, in a stable, a small human being, a child was born this very moment. And the time had come, where he had to talk to the shepherds. Slowly he stood up, and in that second he decided to do it totally differently from the plan. No white wings, no halo, he would just talk.

"I have listened to you," he said, "and I have to tell you something that is really important: Don't be afraid anymore! Don't be afraid of me, of your life, don't be afraid of what the future will hold. For I tell you great joy. In this very night everything has changed. Tonight the saviour is born. Your saviour. And it is happening just around the corner. You don't need to believe me, but you can go and see him for yourselves. Over there, in the little village, in a stable next to the inn, there is a little baby, lying in a manger.

And, like all babies he is wrapped in nappies. This child is here because of you; because God cares. This child is the saviour, the son of the one most high."

It was not his best speech ever, not by far. But it was all he could manage in that moment and he just hoped and prayed that the shepherds would understand him.

At that moment Clarence felt that he was not alone anymore. He could feel the presence of all the other angels even before he could see them. He heard them all
breathe in, and then together sing in many voices the praise of God sounding out into the night, "Glory to God in the highest. And peace on earth among all who God loves."

There they all were, over the field and the flock of sheep: the multitude of the heavenly host, the tall, important arch angels as well as the small soprano angels! And over there, was his whole class, all those angels with whom he had studied to annunciate. They all smiled at him and some gave him a thumbs up, and with their trained voices they again sang it out loudly, "Glory to God in the highest. And peace on earth!"

The Music of the heavens, the eternal praise of the angels filled both the night sky and the earth for this great moment, and it didn't matter anymore if the shepherds could hear them. All that had been needed was for Clarence to speak his words. Clarence understood. He had not been sent to some

28

insignificant task on the side, to announce the birth to some unimportant shepherds. No! He was the Messenger Angel. The only Messenger Angel! What he just had told to the shepherds, that the saviour was born as a little child that was the good news of this holy night for all human beings.

And the shepherds realised that this stranger, who had sat among them and had listened to them and had shared a meal with them, that stranger had spoken the truth. They could not tell why they knew it, but there was something in them that told them, "Yes, it is true what he said".

It was as if the singing of angels filled their heart. They said to each other, "Let us go and see this miracle."

And they packed the little they had and hurried, into the village, to the stable and found the child in a stable, wearing nappies, just like their own children, lying in a manger among the sheep. The child that would change their lives.

So Clarence learned that it is not large crowds that are important. Or the importance of people, or the statistics, or the larger and smaller events, and whether they are in the newspaper the next day or not. What was important was what the good news did in the life of the people. He realised that all that was important was that the good news reached the people so that it could bring warmth in cold nights, and Love where there is hate, community in loneliness and hope in the darkness.

It had gone silent again over the field, by the flock. The angels had returned to heaven to continue to celebrate, a real heavenly party. And Clarence, the messenger angel? Well, he came down the inch and a half he had hovered over the ground. He smiled and watched the shepherds as they walked towards the village, excited and talking to each other. They had totally forgotten about their sheep in all of their excitement. And so he sat down next to the fire, threw a few logs on to it, took the staff and looked over the sleeping flock. Tonight he would watch over the sheep, so that nothing should happen to them while the shepherds would visit their saviour.

What Happened After the Holy Night

I t had become quiet after all the excitement in the stable in Bethlehem. The shepherds had returned to their flock late at night. All of them were rather merry and a little tipsy and so the walked through the otherwise silent Bethlehem, loudly singing songs. How nice of the innkeeper to treat them to a few skins full of wine, so they could toast that little baby in the manger! The three wise ones also had finally retired for the night. With the help of some larger silver coins they had somehow managed to get a room in the otherwise totally sold out city. And they had been so tired and overwhelmed that they didn´t even star a lengthy discussion about the theological implications of what they had just witnessed. And that means something for three wise men who had to share two beds in one room! The innkeeper and his family also went to bed. After all they had to get up early the next morning and work hard, holy night or not. Somebody had to make breakfast for all the guest. Even the choirs and hosts of angles had returned to heaven. They absolutely planned to continue to celebrate in heaven! A party like only the angels in heaven could throw! The star over Bethlehem also dimmed its light. It had done its task and now it, too, wanted to rest.

Only a few little angels remained in the stable. They didn´t want to go to the party of the adult ones. Those grown-ups were so boring. They would just stand around and talk. It would be totally dull. And the little angels knew that they would not give them any of the famous "angelic mullded wine". Which was totally unfair and totally uncool. Even if there was no alcohol in the wine – after all, angels do not need alcohol to celebrate – they would again say: No, you are still too young for that. And then they would send the little angels to bed. But they did not want to go to bed! This was much too exciting for them! They had decided therefor to stay behind secretly while all the other angels flew back to heaven. Actually, it was rather boring: Mary and Joseph did lay in the hay and slept, and the baby slumbered peacefully. Ox and ass just stood there, and nothing happened. And so they played hide and seek and "steal the halo" in the beams of the wooden roof of the stable. They became quite rambunctious, and nearly woke up the child! Suddenly they heard somebody sternly clearing his throat. *Harrumph!*

They had been caught. By one of the big angels. By one of the very big angels. One of those with a white garment and large white wings and bright, holy rays of light. It was the angel of the annunciation himself who had caught them. Now they were in trouble. That much was clear. So the small little band stood there, conscious of their guilt, halos in hand their wings drooping down. The big angel looked down at them with a stern face, shook his head, looked back and sighed. "What shall I do with you?" he said, more to himself and fell silent again. Making the little angels naturally even more nervous.

The big angel sighed again, and said: "Well! Well, since that you are here anyway you can help me." He told them that they should take care of those who had been there that night: The wise ones from far away, the shepherds who had left their flocks and the inn-keeper's family. He himself also had something to do. All the little angels should take with them something from the stable. Some of them would go to the wise ones; some to the shepherds; some would stay here, with the innkeeper and his wife in the inn.

The little angles were happy that they got off without being scolded. And instead they even got an important task to do. This was much better than a boring party in heaven and being sent to bed. They quickly gathered some things that they found in the stable, and flew away as quickly as possible before the big angel could change his mind.

In the morning the wise men woke up in their expensive room in their hotel. And already over breakfast they started to discuss and debate and think and try to understand. After all, they were learned wise men, and wise men do things like that, even at breakfast. And so they invented, at that first morning, words like "incarnational theology". And they had initial thoughts about how something they called "inner-Trinitarian Dialogue" might work. When you, who are reading this, now don´t know what that might mean, do not worry. For the last two thousand years wise men and women have been trying to figure this out, and they are not really far ahead of you. The three wise men, however, suddenly realised, that they did not know how to get home. They had been so focused on following the star, and finding out what the star wanted to tell them, that they didn´t even notice the way they had come. The truth was: They had no clue where they were. Somewhere far away from home, that much was clear. In all their theological discussions they failed to notice their daily progress. They had only gazed at their star. Everything else they had paid for out of their well filled travel purse. Only the goal had been important, and they had found it in the stable. But how to continue now? How to should the get home, without knowing the way?

The little angels who had flown to them clapped their hand in joy. They instantly saw that this was totally their job. They would show the three wise ones a way home and into the future. And what they had gathered in the staple was exactly the thing for that

34

task. They had gathered some of the light of the star. It had sparkled and glittered to beautifully up there in the hole of the roof, like a shiny Christmas ornament. They would use that light to help the three wise men.

Angels, now, can do a lot, but not everything. They cannot, for example, except during the holy night, just ignore the laws of nature. And that night had been a big exception! They cannot just place a star somewhere into the sky, where it does not belong. No, not even angels can do that. They, however, could travel along with the three, carrying the light of the star. They could place a little of it into eyes and hearts of the wise ones and leave traces of it in the world.

And so the wise men suddenly remembered a little part of the way. Not the whole way, that lay still in the darkness of the future or the past, depending on how you want to see it. But they travelled for a whole day, and they found the inn where they had stayed the night before the holy night. And they talked to the people there. That was the first time they did that, in all their travels. They had had such a nice time with those shepherds, why not try it again and talk to ordinary people and listen to what they had to say. And indeed, one of the people there remembered and knew from which direction they had come. And so the wise men could continue the next morning. And so they travelled step by step, day by day, encounter by encounter with people back to their home. It was strange to travel without that larger understanding. But somehow it was as if the star still guided them. Not up there in the sky. But with many little sparkles whenever they met a new person. And one day they came over a hill, that looked familiar, and in front of them was their home. And they had learned a lot on their way.

The other little angles had flown over to the shepherds, just as the angel of the annunciation had told them to do. And they just arrived there in time. It was early in the morning and there was already a lot of shouting and yelling going on. It was not the shepherds who yelled at each other, they were much too tired for that and they had a headache. No, there was a man in very fine clothing with them, who was terribly angry. What were they thinking, to have gone of like that? Leaving his sheep alone? Unbelievable! Unreliable bunch of ... !!! He yelled and called them names! He should fire them, he screamed, all of them! Ungrateful people they were! When he had so generously given them jobs, even in these difficult times, with rising costs and all those Romans about. He kept on and on, and he scolded and insulted them badly.

The first thing the angels wanted to do, they were angels, after all, would be to pour a lot of peace over the man. Then everything would be calm, just as it should be on the first day after the holy night. But then they looked closer. And because angels can see not only the present but also the future, and the can see not only the obvious but also the hidden connections, they saw: a little peace was not enough here. Because what they saw was not only that one man, but the whole story how people are exploited by other people. How some of them struggled in underpaid job, not knowing how to afford their rent, while others became rich. They saw large banks who build large towers, and they saw many people who did not know how to pay their debts at those banks. They saw that the profit of a few became more and more important than the quality of the work No, a little peace was not enough here. But then they smiled at each other. They also had taken something from the staple: the echo of the singing of the angels. And that is what they put into the ears of the shepherds.

And so it happened that the shepherds heard something different, despite the yelling of their boss, an echo from the holy night. They heard "Don´t be afraid!", and "Glory to God in the highest!" It was just a memory, just like you remember a dream, but it was enough. Enough so they gathered together and for the first time stoop up against their boss. First they were very, very careful – after all they still had a headache – but then united and strong. They had not been afraid of the angels, and now they would not be afraid of such people anymore! And the gathered together, demanded a pay rise, and dry wood for their fires and better shepherd´s staffs. And a day off! And the founded the first shepherd´s union and a shepherds co-op to directly marked their sheep and to receive fair prices for their wool. And they realised that to give glory to God also means to treat other people well and with respect. The shepherd business changed funda-mentally. It was still hard work, but they would not be afraid anymore.

The little angels who stayed with the innkeeper and his wife had to wait the longest time for their moment to come. Winter changed into spring, and into summer and autumn. And finally autumn became winter again. The work at the inn continued as always, business was average and the days were filled with a lot of work and now and then a festive day. There was nothing the little angels had to take care of. It was just about the same time as last year, that the angels realised that something was wrong. Now, angels can see thing that humans only can feel. And the saw that the world around the innkeepers family had become grey. They had not seen this earlier, but now they saw it clearly: Everything was grey, and dull. It was routine, daily live, the same every day. It was getting up, go to work and eat and sleep. And then again sleep, eat and work. And the more grey life became, the more unfriendly people were. They did not really fight, no, they just stopped to talk meaningfully with each other. The daily chores were discussed, but not those things that are really important.

And even themselves, the little angels realised, had become more grey. Their little wings were not white anymore, but light grey, just like curtains, who had not been washed properly in a long time. Even their halos did not shine properly, anymore. They even realised, that they had not sung any songs in a long time! It was high time to do something! And so they unpacked what they had gathered in that night a year before: the joy that had been in the air, because people had come together and the angels had sung to celebrate the birth of the saviour. That joy they unpacked, and scattered it
all over the inn, put it into every corner and hung it into every window and let it shine from every candle.

All at once there was something in the air, something special. The innkeeper and his wife could not really say what it was, but they decided, in that moment, to have a celebration. There was no real reason for it, but then they remembered: It must have been about a year ago, when this child was born, over there, in the stable. It had been such a nice night, and so they decided to do it right again: They invited their family and the neighbours, and yes, those shepherds should come, too. What might have happened to the little boy and his parents? And what of those three foreign men who had brought presents. Presents, well, that was a nice idea. Of course, not gold and frankincense, but something nice and small for the children and socks for the innkeeper. It was a cheerful, colourful celebration that lasted until late that night. They sat together, there was plenty to eat and drink and they sang songs. Somehow it was as if the joy and the holiness of that night had come back to them. And angels, who again hovered over the inn radiated in bright light and they knew: they wanted to celebrate such a joyful feast every year from now on. A feast that interrupts the daily routine and reminds people of the joy of that one special night.

Now you might ask, what the big angel did. Perhaps you think that he gave Josef the dream, so he and Mary and Jesus could flee to Egypt. Or you think that he even went along to protect them on their dangerous journey. But that were the tasks of a dream angel and of a lot of guardian angels. The big angel had a task that was much more difficult and it would take much longer. Again he sighed, took a deep breath and removed his bright white garment. Underneath he wore normal human cloth, just as you would wear it every day. After he had tucked his wings under the shirt, only his bright halo gave away that he was an angel. He took the halo from where it hovered just over his head, carefully folded it and put it in the pocket of his trousers. He didn´t need to take anything from the stable. All he needed he already had. And so he took off, the angel of annunciation who just had become the angel of peace. Because this was what he, the big angel, had to do: to tell the people what the angels had sung: Peace on earth and goodwill to all!

But now it is true that it took all the heavenly host raising their voices together on that one very special and holy night, to have been able for people to have heard and seen them.

And so the angel of peace, in the disguise of an ordinary human being, took a different approach: He would explain to people again and again, what peace really is. He would be a many peace rallies and hold signs in the air. Every now and then he would be invited to mediate between people, small and large. He would whisper "peace!" into their ears and sing about the Shalom of God. That peace, that happened in that long ago night in Bethlehem. He knew that his task was big and that he would need a lot of time. But being an angel he had the patience that was necessary. That is why the angel who announces peace is still among us, dressed as an ordinary person. And who knows: perhaps he is right here today.

And the small angels, you might ask? They, too, are still somewhere here in our world. They had so much left over from what they had gathered in the stable: light of the star over Bethlehem that gives a direction in life; songs of the angels that gives courage to heal the world; and joy over a birth and something new that changes everything. When you are quiet and listen and look carefully you can see the light of the star, and hear the words of the angels. And when we celebrate, a feast where all are invited, then there is hope. A hope for peace in our hearts and in the world.

How it Came that the Little Soprano
Angels sang over the Manger

Presents, there should be presents for the birth of the Son of God. That, the angels agreed on. And therefore, there was a lot of excitement in heaven, in the time before Christmas. Everywhere they tinkered and worked, everywhere the angels tried to have the best idea, tried to come up with the best, the greatest, the most beautiful idea.

They would send one of them down, with a huge bag, filled with presents and he should then use the presents of the angels to prepare a place, where the Son of the Almighty would be born. Beautiful, this place would be, and warm, and peaceful and filled with the most wonderful music. Yes, and it should smell good, that was important! And so the angels built and packed: Warmth that came directly from the Spring sunshine; the colours of the rainbow and the beauty of nature filled with light; a large portion of the peace that fills the heavens, and the heavenly fragrance from the kitchen of the angels. And a lot of music: notes and rhythms and chords sounds in many voices, and short breaks that make the music interesting.

All that the angels packed and put it into the large bag, which their messenger angel would take along.

Only the little soprano angels, the smallest and youngest of all angels didn't know quite what they should give. They were still so small and young and so far they only knew one song, and that song they still had to practice. And so they did not have a lot of time to work on their present. But they had an idea. They would go over to the cloud where the tools and the left overs from creation were in storage. That cloud was their favourite playground anyhow, because they always found so many interesting things there. Some of the sound of the waves, half a tree that wasn't used, the eruption of a volcano that didn't get finished, the fragrance of lilies of the valley, just stuff like that.

And here they found the present which they thought would fit: a little bit humanity, left over from creation.

The grown up angels tried to not laugh out loud, when they saw the small, insignificant and plain little gift. It was so insignificant in comparison to their presents. But because they were adults, and knew how to deal with children, they patted them on their little halos, put the present on the very bottom of the bag, and sent the soprano angels back to choir rehearsal.

That the Almighty on the throne had seen this present with special interest, and had nodded approvingly, they did not see in all of the Christmas stress and in their pride of their beautiful and expensive presents.

And why the Creator only smiled knowingly whenever they showed him another of the presents, but otherwise was surprisingly quiet, that the angels didn't understand either.

And so the messenger - angel started, shortly before the night, when the miracle was due to happen. He had his big bag with all the angels' presents with him.

But now, the way out of the heavens and eternity down to earth and into time is long and far. The angel was able to fly very fast, but still he had to cross time and space. And on his way the angel came by a lot of situations and saw a lot of people. At the beginning he didn't look too closely, but after a while he started to notice what was happening around him. And so he slowed down, and finally stopped. It wasn't a beautiful place to stop. All around him there was battle and war. The angel was hurt to see how the humans fought and hurt each other. And because angels are in their very nature deeply good beings, he opened his bag and took out a little of the peace, that fills the heavens. Nobody would miss such a tiny amount. And he placed it on his hand and blew it over the battle. And he watched, as the humans stopped, laid down their arms and saw in the other, in the enemy, the fellow human being. And he flew on.

Then he saw somebody, who was totally alone, lonely. It was cold around this person, because she did not have anybody to keep her warm. And the angel took a little of the warmth of the Spring sunshine and poured it over her, and she felt that warmth in the embrace of a friend. And he flew on.

And he saw a man, who had lost everything and his faith through the cruelty of men, and who was desperate and hopeless. And he gave him notes and chords and sounds and texts, so that he would write songs, so glorious and beautiful, that even centuries later people would sing: "Amazing grace, how sweet the sound". And he flew on.

And again and again the angel stopped and placed a little of the presents of the angels in the situations of the world. There were so much of those presents. The little that he gave away, nobody would miss, surely. A little of the fragrance of the heavenly kitchen in a house, that became open and hospitable. A little beauty in the eye of someone, that created love in the heart. And again and again: a little peace, a little warmth.

Actually, the angel felt very bad. After all, it was the presents of the angels for the newborn Son of God he was giving away so freely. But surely, he reassured himself, it was only a little he gave away, and there was so much more. And nobody would ever notice. Still, it did not feel quite right. But every time, the angel reached into the bag and took out some of the presents to give them away, he had the strong feeling, that God smile on the heavenly throne. And then the angel felt much better.

It was late at night, when the angel finally reached the little village, Bethlehem, where the miracle was about to happen. It was freezing cold, and it got dark quickly. On the way, not very far from the village, he had passed the young couple. It was clear that they were very tired, and as far as the angel could tell, it was not much longer to the big moment. He would have to hurry, if he wanted to prepare everything - nice and warm and peaceful for the birth.

And so the angel placed his bag on the ground, opened it up ready to start his preparations. But he experienced the biggest shock of his angel existence: The bag was empty. All the presents, all the beauties, all the warmth, all the light, all was gone. All was given away. He hadn't realised that he had given away so much. Nothing was left. How should he now build a place in which the Son of the Almighty could be born? How should he fulfil his task to find a place for the birth? Even if he had money – which angels do not have in the first place – one glance into the village showed him: There was no room, not an empty bed anywhere. Everything was sold out! In despair the angel sat down on the corner of a street, and let his wings hang down. In a few minutes the young couple would come up the street and he had failed. Even if he could fly back and collect all the angels' presents it was too late. How could he let himself be seen in heaven ever again? How should he face the Creator? And, after all, why had the Almighty not stopped him from acting so foolishly? The angel was angry with himself and pitied himself.

Suddenly he saw something in the bag. At the very bottom of it, deep down, there was something. Something small and insignificant.

As the angel looked, he found it. It was the present of the little soprano angels: A little bit of humanity, left over from creation. The wild hope, which had started to break out in the angel, died again. What on earth should he do with that? Useless present of childish angels. He watched the couple that came up the road, went from door to door and knocked, and was sent away from every door. Only too soon there was only one inn left, and they were sold out too. They would be sent away again, the angel knew it. But in that moment he knew what he could do. And so he flew, with that little bit of humanity in his hand on silent angel wings into the inn. And he placed this little bit of humanity into the heart of the innkeeper.

The innkeeper heard somebody knock on the door, on the evening of that frantic day. And first he wanted to shout at the couple, and the young woman heavily pregnant, to make things worse! "We are sold out", and "go away", he had wanted to grumble. But then, something strange had happened. Deep down in his heart something had touched him, something had happened and so he said: "Yes, there is a place in the stable; I will bring something warm to eat and some blankets … and something to wrap the small one in, when it comes."

It was cold in the stable, which was really only a hut, built next to the inn, nothing more. It was crooked, windy, smelly and ugly. But somehow the angel had the strong feeling that it was right, the way it was. And he stood there as Mary gave birth to her firstborn son, just as he had told her nine months earlier.

In heaven the angels had watched all of this. They wanted to interfere, wanted to stop him from giving away everything. They wanted to shout out loud, they wanted to do something! With their wings they covered their eyes, and they tore at their angel hair, and bit into their halos, they were so nervous. But God on the throne strictly forbade them to intervene. The angels didn't understand it. And even less they understood, that God nodded approvingly, every time the angel on earth had given something away. And he smiled! It would be a catastrophe, they thought and there was a breathless silence in the last minutes before the birth in the stable. A silence, which was broken by the overflowing joy of God, as the Creator saw, what the angel did with the gift of humanity.

And suddenly there was excitement in the heavenly throne room! The little soprano angels should come, and they should fly, fast as the wind and the light and the joy, fly down to the manger, and they should sing, should sing what they had practised. And Godself showed them the shortcut that started right behind the throne and lead directly to the stable, and the little angels flew as fast as their little wings carried them and they gathered over the stable and they sang, like no angels had sung ever before. They sang the glory of the one who was born in the stable, the one who would be called Immanuel, God with us, and they sang: "Glory to God in the highest and peace to all people on earth." And their song sounded, as the shepherds came, and the foreign wise ones, and many people to adore him.

And so it happened, that the stable was cold and windy, and that Jesus lay in a manger and not in a palace, built by the angels, and that the little soprano angels sang the Glory of God, in that night in Bethlehem.

But what happened to the angels' presents, you might ask? Well, he had travelled a very long way, through time and space, and he had given away a lot. And when we look out today and admire the beauty of the sky and the sunset and the rainbow, when we hear the Creator's praise in the melody of a Christmas song, when we smell a meal, to which friends and strangers are invited, when we feel the warmth of an embrace when we feel lonely and are cold, then we experience a little bit of the presents of the angels.

The most important present of all, though, the present, that changed all and turned it to the best in the end, that was the present of the little soprano angels: A little bit humanity, that opens our eyes and our hearts to the need and the poorness of others and gives us the strength to open the doors in our world.

This present I wish for all of us, more than all other presents in this world for Christmas.

How the Little Angel and the Little Star Tried to Find the Perfect Place For the Birth

Nobody had any time for the two of them. Nobody wanted to play with them. Again and again they heard: "Get out of my way! Can´t you play somewhere else? Please, can you be a little more quiet? I have to concentrate!" And nobody wanted to let them help, either!

It was so unfair! Just because they were still so small they never were allowed to help, when something exciting happened. The big angels were all mean! The little angel and the small star were offended. And now they were sitting on a cloud somewhere away from the general excitement and watched as the big angels turned all of heaven upside down planning and working and tinkering.

Big Angels are stupid. The little angel and the small star totally agreed on that. They practically always agreed on everything.. Since they met, some eternity ago they were the best of friends. They were inseparable, especially when it was about doing some kind of nonsense somewhere in heaven. But now it all was too hectic and exhilarating and they did not feel up to any shenanigans.

They wanted to help, that's what they wanted! "This is such an important time", they had heard again and again from the big angels, and "Everything needs to be perfect and wonderful!" The two of them did not really understand exactly what important thing was about to happen. "It is just before Christmas" the big angels would say, and they were all totally beside themselves. It had to be something brand new, but the little angel and the small star did not really understand the complicated explanation of the Head-theologian-angel. Christmas was all about the "Incarnation", he had said, as if that would make any sense.

Anyhow, it was sheer chaos in heaven so shortly before Christmas, THE Christmas, the very first, original Christmas. Soon it would happen that the son of God would be born a human among humans on earth. The heavenly hosts could not wait for the day, since it became known that the day was just about to happen. And now it was only a few weeks away. Not that time was of any issue in heaven. But well informed circles reported that just today the archangel Gabriel himself was on a somehow secret mission down on earth, to take care of the most important preparation of all.

From now it would be exactly nine months until the birth. The older angels who heard that rumor, nodded knowingly and wise, and agreed. But whenever the little angel asked what that meant, they blushed and got all embarrassed and did not want to explain those nine months. And the large stars and planets and suns also just sparkled secretively. The small star had become burning red, so infuriated was he, but he still did not get any answer. The only thing they found out was, that somehow God himself wanted to go down to earth. He would be born just like a human and would live, for a short while, among them. And they also understood that this was something unheard of and reason enough for a big celebration.

Everywhere in heaven one could see smaller and larger groups of angels flying around in excited discussions. Of course, there was only one subject: the birth of the savior and how and where it would happen and how and where it would be celebrated. Everybody agreed that this would be the biggest birthday party since the creation of earth. What the angels did not agree on were basically all other details of the planed festivities. Every angel had plans and ideas:

The heavenly composer angels had already retreated to a remote cloud and were busy to compose: several Birthday-hymns, a Birthday-Oratory and at least one Birthday-symphony. The angels who were in charge of experimental modern music had grouped up with the special-effects angels and worked with the thunder of creation, celestial sounds and the choir of animal voices with the full cast of Noah's Ark. The general opinion, though, was that this piece of music was not really suited for the birth of a small child.

Much more controversial were the discussion about where the performance would take place. One option was a simultaneous broadcast to every temple, shrine and holy place all over the globe. Another option was to send small groups into each and every village, town and city in Israel. The little angel had tried to sneak into the rehearsals, but they had discovered him immediately, and had thrown them out. They would not even let him play the triangle! He had been close to tears!

The heavenly head office for stars and other shiny objects had some ideas that truly would be spectacular: The stars in heaven as a brilliant firework, accompanied by a music for fireworks by the heavenly orchestra. Comets and fixed stars would shine and fly and dance for the birth, and then, as the grand finale, would write the name of the Son of God in high, burning letters onto the sky! It would be a ballet of the stars! But the little star had already been told, that he was much too small for that. And no, he could not even be in the last row, he would just mess up things. With bent down rays he flew away, thinking very unkind and un-star like thoughts about big stars!

The Union of heavenly keepers of the animals had heated discussion about the list of wild and domestic animals that should appear after the birth, bringing the adoration of nature to the newborn son of men. There would not have been such a conference of the animals since Noah´s arc and the gathering of the creatures there. The logistic problems would be immense and perhaps they would have to hire extra helpers to organize that all.

While all this was happening, the little angel and the small star sat together on their cloud and sulked. They had told each other how the adult stars and angels just refused to let them help, up here in heaven. They had agreed, as they always did, that those adults were… well, so adult! It was a child that was about to be born, down on earth. And the two of them should be totally involved in all that planning. After all, they were the experts for children here. What did adults know about children? They were all so busy arranging things here in heaven and nobody thought about the child that would be born down there, somewhere, wherever that was.

They looked at each other. As always, they had the same thought. What a brilliant idea! It would be a great adventure! Let the adults do what they wanted. The two, the little angel and the small star would fly down to earth and find the best, the most beautiful, safest, most wonderful and absolutely perfect place, where the little child, the son of the most high, could be born. Yes, that's what they would do. And then they would come back and show that place to the adult angels and the big stars. Everybody would be thrilled and would praise them for doing such an important part of the preparation, something nobody had thought about.

In all that hectic commotion it had been no problem for the two of them to sneak out of heaven. During one of their games they had found one of the hidden entrances to heaven, so they did not even had to use the pearly gates. They just squeezed through a little crack in between some clouds and quickly flew over to earth. Nobody had seen them, great! They had not remembered, though, that God on the heavenly throne saw everything. But God would not tell on them, but rather, he smiled silently while he was watching them. Even angels and stars sometimes forget, that God always has a loving eye on everybody.

Wow, this earth was big! They had been used to the infinity of the heaven, but this earth, now that was something else! There was so much so see, so many places and days and hours! Now it is a fact that angels in heaven live in God's eternity and outside of our time. This is the reason why they not only can fly from one place to the other, but also from one time to the next. And stars have a totally different concept of time altogether. Days and hours are much so small pieces of times for stars, who think in millions of years. And so the little angel and the small star were soon lost in the world and in the time.

But that did not matter! Down here it was so great, and there was so much to explore. Surely there would not be a problem to find a just perfect space and a great, wonderful time where and when the birth could take place.

It wasn´t as easy, as they had imagined though. One of the first places they stopped already seemed, on first sight, really good. It was bright and clean and warm, and a lot of people where there, too. That would be quite important, the little angel thought. After all, the people on earth should notice what would happen. Yes, this place was good. There was even some nice background music, he liked that. And the small star liked the place, too. He flew through the place and watched his light and sparkle be reflected in many ornaments and garlands and objects made from glass. A perfect place for a little child. They agreed: they had already found the perfect place.

But then they had a second glance at the people in this place. Somehow it was just as in heaven: a lot of running and hectic and preparations for something. None of the big people seemed to have time for the little ones. Which was strange, after all the big ones always said that they would do this just for the little ones and they would buy presents just for them. The little angel sensed a lot of frustration and worries in a world that was too fast and complicated, not only for angles, but for the people, too. He would see on the faces of the people that they lived in a constant competition. Who would buy the best, the most expensive, the most impressive present? Already now they thought about something they called "exchanging things after the holidays" and they dreaded the day when they had to come back to the shopping center. The closer the little angel and the small star watched, the more they saw, that this was not a good place for a birth, after all. No, not here.

It was the small star, who found a much better place. It was wonderful, all tranquility and peace. Deep snow covered the trees, and his light filled the icicles with light and the snowflakes with glitter. When he tried really hard he could paint colorful patterns onto the snow-white snow. The mountain ranges glowed in heavenly colors. A silent, peaceful night lay over the snowy forest and the little angel was thrilled, too. Being an angel he could hear the music of the night, the sound of silence and the rhythm of quietness. It was so beautiful and for a while he just sat there, holding his breath and listened through the night.

But after they sat there for a while they realized that something were missing. There was nobody there, nobody at all. The little angel was the first who realized: there would be always people who would retreat into solitude, who would be able to hear the music of creation in the silence. Some few would come and search for God in the peace of nature. But is would be precious few who would really do and not only talk about it. Like angels and stars people liked to be in community with each other. So the birth would have to happen in a place where people could come to.

They continued their search and looked for places where many people came together. Again and again they found the same problem. Everywhere where many people came together it was loud and hectic and confusing. Or, even worse, it became aggressive. Neither the small star nor the little angel could understand that: wherever a lot of people gathered, they started a fight. It was strange: they were so different from each other. They had so many colors and forms and ways of live. But instead of rejoicing in that diversity, they gathered in small groups of people who were rather similar.

And then they started a fight with another group of people, just because that group looked or smelled or talked a little different, or wore different clothes than the others. Practically everywhere where the two of them went, they found such fights. Sometimes it was only little fights, like the people in one house against the people in the house next door. Often enough there were big fights, though. Many people would fight with each other with violence and weapons. More than once the little angel and the little star had just escaped, the angel with ruffled feathers in his wings and the star with broken rays of light.

Even in places where people wanted to concentrate especially on God, where they sang and prayed and tried to listen to God, the little angel and the small star found the same mistrust and the same fear. It was little different in those holy places. The two did not understand those people: they had all those opportunities, could do so much. They could love each other like the angels do, and they could shine and sparkle like stars. And sometimes they even did it. Those were precious, special moments. Yet again and again fear and mistrust and stress and fighting started among them.

Finally the two of them sat, downcast and disheartened under a tree in a country where God had spoken often to the people. So many prophets, men and women alike, had heard God's word and had told the people about God. But even here it was not better than anywhere else. Quite the contrary: Here, where the land should be holy, it was often worse. They had looked through time. During practically every time in history, there were armies marching and people had to flee from bad people who had the power and wanted to suppress people.

Or they took refuge in this country, because they had to flee, but instead of learning from it, they often did the same to others. And even when there were no armies, who fought, then the people hated each other. Just because some believed a little different in God than the others did. They did not even grant each other the possibility that God might love the other, too. As if God did not have love enough for everybody! They were broken hearted.

The little angel let his wings hang down and the light of the star became dull and he ceased to glitter. Suddenly it became bright all around them. One of the very big angels stood there. O-oh... they had been caught. And to make things worse, it was Gabriel, the head-arch-angel himself. Surly they were in trouble now! But after what they head heard and had seen down here on earth, things could not get worse.

They were very surprised when Gabriel smiled warmly at them instead of scolding them. "Hey, the two of you," he said, "why are you sitting here, looking so sad? We have been watching everything in heavenly throne room. And tell you what: we had never really planned to do the birth of the savior the way most angels wanted it to be. Oh, those angels!" He laughed. "They will never learn that the humans are so totally different than we are in heaven. Up there, in heaven, everything is perfect and wonderful and peaceful, even when we all are gathered together. Down here on earth it is different. So we were really glad when we saw that you two flew down to see earth directly. You have seen a lot, haven´t you? And you did not find a perfect, heavenly, angelic place?"

The little angel nodded and the small star glittered once affirmative. They had looked so hard, everywhere, but had found nothing. Instead they sat right here, in this time and at this place. Perfect was something different! "Precisely here and today it will happen!!" Gabriel said. Here? And today? The angel and the star looked at each other. It was dark and cold. The times were dangerous; people had to flee their homes; soldiers had the power; and an evil king reigned over the land. The people did believe something, yes, but their faith was again and again interrupted by doubts and hesitations and faintheartedness. Even the weather was dismal. It was winter. One of those ugly, grey and wet and rainy winters, when the cold seeps into your bones, not one of the bright, and brisk snowy winters that had looked so beautiful up in the high mountains. This was the place where God wanted to be born? Seriously?

"Seriously." Gabriel answered. "You know, God wants to be with the people, which means, God has to be where the people are. In their places and times and in their realities, and sometimes in the middle of the night. But this night will be a Holy Night. That's why we need you both. You have seen the world in all her beauty and with all her problems. And now you will go and invite people to this Holy Night. I am certain that you can do that. You know, whom to invite." He laughed, one of this clear, bright angel-laughters. "You know, we adult ones are sometimes so busy with our own plans.....Sometimes we are so afraid that the celebration, we angels have planed, will not work out. So we decided to leave it to you children to decide who shall come the feast. Do you see that stable, over there? That's the place where the savior is to be born, this very moment. Now, hurry up and collect all those you want to invite!"

The little angel and the little star looked at each other: Really? They should organize the birthday-party? Seriously? Obviously Gabriel meant what he had said, he had already returned to heaven. But it did not matter, the two of them knew exactly what they wanted to do.

As always they agreed without words. And so the little star flew through the time and far away. He would search for three wise men, which he would call. It would be tree wise kings, from a foreign country. First of all, so they could bring presents. One can´t celebrate a birthday without presents! But most important was that they would follow his light, and not some words. They would have to learn that sometimes one has to follow surprising paths; that sometimes there is only the light of a star, and not deep knowledge. The wise kings would have the adventure of a lifetime and they would find God, among Gods people. Ah, it would be so funny to see the faces of the three wise men, when they finally would understand. The little star started to shine and sparkle bright and beautifully in anticipation.

The little angel also knew where to go. He just flew over to some shepherds, who kept watch over their flocks by night. And because he was so confident in what he wanted to do, some of the security and the joy of the angels and of heaven was with him. He would not say a lot. Just that they should not be afraid. And that they could come, just as they were. With everything they would bring along: all their hopes and joys as well as all their questions, their doubts, and their conflicts. He would not ask them to leave anything behind. They would understand that God had come to them, and with that, to all the people on earth. They would talk about it and some people would understand what that means: That no worries were necessary and no preparations. They did not need to change the whole world, because this birth alone was the change. Through the birth of God into the world, there would be peace, again and again, regardless of how often people would start to fight. They would feel that this night would be a holy night, even if it would not look like the pictures on Christmas-greeting-cards. It was a holy night because it was an ordinary night in the world of the people.

And so the little angel and the little star ended up right there in the middle of the great celebration of the first Christmas. They were there with the shepherds and the wise kings. They hovered over the stable and the manger with all the other angels. The joined in with the singing of the angels and the stars. And they knew, they sang because of the birth of the savior, but also because there were people there: shepherds who were not afraid in the night and wise men who had followed a star. Shepherds who would later leave with songs on their hearts and in their voices and wise men who had enough trust to listen to a dream.

And so they all joined into the song that resounds in heaven and could be heard on earth that night: Glory to God in the highest and peace on earth, goodwill to all.

About the Author

Rev. Dr. Axel Schwaigert, born 1968, is the founding pastor of Salz der Erde Metropolitan Community Church in Stuttgart, Germany. He Doctor of Ministry degree at Episcopal Divinity School in Cambridge, MA. He has been a member of the MCC Theologies Team from its beginning in 2006 and served as a member of the Commission on the MCC Statement of Faith.

He received his Diplom in Evangelisch Theologie (Diploma in Protestant Theology) from the School of Theological Studies at Tubingen (Germany) and studied inter-religious dialogue at Temple University in Philadelphia, PA. He began his pastoral training in 1998 at MCC Bournemouth. After his ordination in 2000 he launched the new Salz der Erde MCC Stuttgart during Gay Pride.

In his secular life, Rev. Schwaigert works as a funeral director. He loves singing, dancing, and acting on stage in musicals, which he sometimes dares at a community theater of the US Forces in Stuttgart.